I Love Swimming Lessons

An Ivy and Mack story

Written by Juliet Clare Bell

Illustrated by Gustavo Mazali

with Adrienn Greta Schönberg

Collins

What's in this story?

Listen and say

jump

splash

swim

It was Saturday and Ivy and Mack had swimming lessons at the sports centre.

"I love swimming lessons," said Ivy.

"Me too," said Mack.

Dad took them to the sports shop.
Mack needed a new swimsuit.

"You grow very fast!" said Dad.
"Which one would you like?"

"*This* one, please! I *love* the colours!"
said Mack.

"Wow!" said Mack. "It's *The Big Jump*!"

"It looks fantastic," said Ivy.

"Can we do this, Dad?" asked Mack. "Please?"

"I'm sorry, but your swimming lesson is starting now," said Dad.

"But I don't want to *swim* now," said Mack. "I want to *jump*!"

"Ivy, do you think we can go on *The Big Jump* after swimming?" asked Mack.

"I don't know," said Ivy. "I don't think there are any more tickets."

"Ok," said the swimming teacher. "Let's start!"

Ivy and Mack swam to the side of the pool. They saw splashing.

"Look, Mack!" said Ivy. "That boy is wearing the same swimsuit as you!"

"That's funny," said Mack.

The boy jumped into the pool. There was a big splash.

It was the end of the lesson.

"Well done, everyone," said the instructor.
"You have ten minutes to play,"

"Yes!" said Mack. "Let's play ball, Ivy!"

Then the boy jumped into the swimming pool again. He was next to Mack. Mack got very wet. The water went in his eyes.

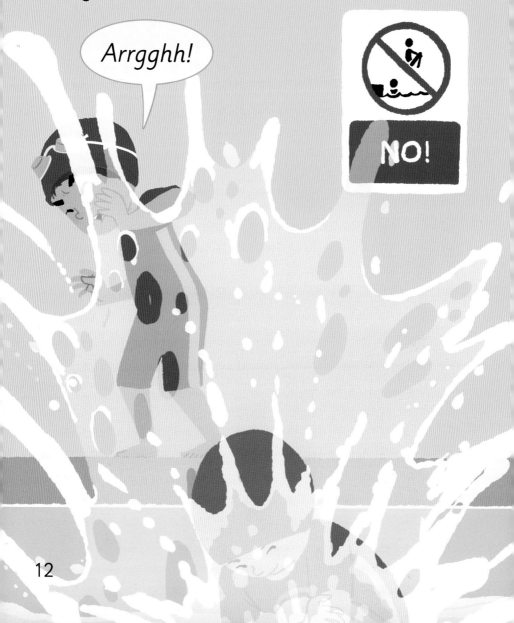

"Are you OK, Mack?" asked Ivy.

"That boy splashed me!" said Mack.

One of the lifeguards talked to Mack.

"Stop!" he said to Mack. "Look at the poster! It's not safe!"

"I don't understand," said Mack.

"But he …" said Ivy.

"I saw you jump into the pool. You can't do that. Now get out of the pool."

"But it was a different boy!" said Mack.

"It *was* a different boy," said Ivy.

"I saw you!" said the lifeguard. "Please get out."

NO!

Mack got out of the pool.

"I'm coming with you, Mack," said Ivy.

"It's OK, Ivy," said Mack. "You can play in the pool."

"No, I'm coming with you!" said Ivy.

Mack saw Dad in front of the changing rooms.

"Are you OK, Mack?" asked Dad.

"A boy jumped into the pool and the lifeguard thinks it was Mack," said Ivy.

"Oh no!" said Dad.

"It was a different boy, Dad!" said Mack.
"The lifeguard made a mistake," said Ivy.
"I know," said Dad. "Don't worry, Mack.
Let's get dressed and go home. We can
watch a film with Mum."

"I'm very sorry," said the lifeguard. "I got the wrong boy. These tickets are for you."

Mack was happy. "*The Big Jump*! Wow, thank you!" he said.

"We've got tickets," said Mack to the woman at the door.

The woman smiled. "That's great," she said. "Have fun."

Ivy and Mack jumped and jumped on *The Big Jump*. "I love *The Big Jump*," said Mack.

A boy came up to Mack. He looked at Mack's T-shirt. "Look, we've got the same T-shirt," he said.

"Not again!" said Mack.

Picture dictionary

Listen and repeat

changing room

lifeguard

sports centre

swimming lesson

swimming pool

swimsuit

1 Look and order the story

2 Listen and say

Collins

Published by Collins
An imprint of HarperCollins*Publishers*
Westerhill Road
Bishopbriggs
Glasgow
G64 2QT

HarperCollins*Publishers*
1st Floor, Watermarque Building
Ringsend Road
Dublin 4
Ireland

William Collins' dream of knowledge for all began with the publication of his first book in 1819.

A self-educated mill worker, he not only enriched millions of lives, but also founded a flourishing publishing house. Today, staying true to this spirit, Collins books are packed with inspiration, innovation and practical expertise. They place you at the centre of a world of possibility and give you exactly what you need to explore it.

© HarperCollins*Publishers* Limited 2020

10 9 8 7 6 5 4 3 2

ISBN 978-0-00-839834-7

Collins® and COBUILD® are registered trademarks of HarperCollins*Publishers* Limited

www.collins.co.uk/elt

British Library Cataloguing in Publication Data

A catalogue record for this publication is available from the British Library.

Author: Juliet Clare Bell
Lead illustrator: Gustavo Mazali (Beehive)
Copy illustrator: Adrienn Greta Schönberg (Beehive)
Series editor: Rebecca Adlard
Publishing manager: Lisa Todd
Product managers: Jennifer Hall and Caroline Green
In-house editor: Alma Puts Keren
Project manager: Emily Hooton
Editor: Deborah Friedland
Proofreaders: Natalie Murray and Michael Lamb
Cover designer: Kevin Robbins
Typesetter: 2Hoots Publishing Services Ltd
Audio produced by id audio, London
Reading guide author: Julie Penn
Production controller: Rachel Weaver
Printed and bound by: GPS Group, Slovenia

MIX
Paper from
responsible sources

FSC
www.fsc.org

FSC™ C007454

Download the audio for this book and a reading guide for parents and teachers at www.collins.co.uk/839834